JUNE 30,th JUNE 30th

Books by Richard Brautigan

Novels

Trout Fishing in America
A Confederate General from Big Sur
In Watermelon Sugar
The Abortion: An Historical Romance 1966
The Hawkline Monster: A Gothic Western
Willard and His Bowling Trophies:
    A Perverse Mystery
Sombrero Fallout: A Japanese Novel
Dreaming of Babylon: A Private Eye Novel 1942

Poetry

The Galilee Hitch-Hiker*
Lay the Marble Tea*
The Octopus Frontier*
All Watched Over by Machines of Loving Grace*
Please Plant This Book
The Pill Versus the Springhill Mine Disaster
Rommel Drives on Deep into Egypt
Loading Mercury with a Pitchfork
June 30th, June 30th

Short Stories

Revenge of the Lawn

*out of print

JUNE 30,th
JUNE 30th

Richard Brautigan

DELACORTE PRESS/SEYMOUR LAWRENCE

Published by
Delacorte Press/Seymour Lawrence
1 Dag Hammarskjold Plaza
New York, New York 10017

Lines from *Sappho: A New Translation*. Translated by Mary Barnard. Published in 1958 by The Regents of the University of California; reprinted by permission of the University of California Press.

Page viii is reproduced from *Bungaku Kai*, Autumn 1976, by permission of the publisher, Kodansha Ltd.

One of the poems in this volume first appeared in *Quest/77* magazine.

Manufactured in the United States of America

First printing

Designed by MaryJane DiMassi

Library of Congress Cataloging in Publication Data

Brautigan, Richard.
    June 30th, June 30th.

    I. Title.
PS3503.R2736J8 1978   811'.5'4   77-26782
ISBN 0-440-04295-X

This book is for Shiina Takako.
"my Japanese sister"
Calle de Eternidad

文 學 界

11 月 号

ディキンスンのロシア語　　長谷川四郎

こないだ六本木のクレードルで壁にもたれた
ブローティガンにひょっこり
会ったらぼそぼそ言ってた
エミリ・ディキンスンを
サンフランシスコの安アパートの
ラジエーターのパイプの曲りにはめこんどいたら
冬になると口笛吹いてホチーチェルイバとやるんだが
ホチーチェルイバってなんのことかな

サラトフのホテルで
朝にマクシム・ゴーリキーが目をさますと
窓際のスチームが「お魚はいかが」
――ホチーチェルイバと呼びかけるそうだ

それはよいことをきいた
とブローティガンは指を鳴らした
エミリ・ディキンスンが
ロシヤ語を話すとは知らなかったよ

DICKINSON'S RUSSIAN

BY HASEGAWA SHIRŌ

I ran into Richard Brautigan recently.
He was slumped against the wall
In the Roppongi bar Cradle.
He mumbled:
"You know, I jammed Emily Dickinson
Between the pipes of my radiator in San Francisco,
And in the winter she whistles, 'Hochitse-ryba!'
I wonder what it could mean?"

In his hotel in Saratov,
Maxim Gorki would awake in the morning
To the steam pipes by the window calling,
Hochitse-ryba!
"Would you like fish?"

"Thanks for telling me!"
Cried Brautigan, snapping his fingers.
"I didn't know Emily Dickinson could speak
    Russian!"

translated by Kazuko Fujimoto Goodman

INTRODUCTION:

Farewell, Uncle Edward, and All the Uncle Edwards

My uncle Edward is dead.

He died when he was twenty-six years old.

He was the pride of my family.

The year was 1942.

Indirectly he was killed by the people of Japan, waging war against the people of the United States of America. That was a long time ago.

He was on Midway Island working as an engineer when the Japanese attacked the island on December 7, 1941. Warplanes began strafing and bombing. My uncle Edward was handed a machine gun to help defend the island. He saw a good place to set up the gun and started toward it. He was never to arrive at that place.

There was an explosion nearby from a Japanese bomb casting, like a shadow, shrapnel into his head. Everything went blank for my uncle Edward and the place where he was headed to set up the machine gun went very faraway and dark and had nothing to do with his life any more.

He was evacuated from Midway by ship and taken to Hawaii where he remained unconscious in a coma for months. The shrapnel was removed from his head and he lay there asleep week after week with his head wrapped in bandages until after a long time his eyes opened and he was returned to this world again, but it was not for long.

He was to partially recover from his December 7th wounds during the spring of 1942 and die later in the year, working on a "secret" air base in Sitka, Alaska.

He spent his recovery period in Hawaii writing poetry in the vein of Rudyard Kipling, Robert W. Service and Omar Khayyam. Also, he copied from memory poems by them. They were among his effects that my mother ended up with. He had been a brilliant engineer and something of a romantic besides.

The poems were in three-ring spiral notebooks.

I remember reading them in the years just after the war. It gave me a strange feeling to read them. The war was over. We had won. My uncle Edward was dead and I was reading his poetry.

After he got out of the hospital in Honolulu he went to San Francisco and had a two-week love affair with a divorcée. That was a big thing in those days. Their common bond other than obvious physical pleasure was a deep affection for the poetry of Omar Khayyam which they would quote to each other, hopefully after making fantastic love together.

I think my uncle Edward deserved that for he had just a few more months to live. He would be dead in the autumn. I would be standing beside his coffin in the form of a seven-year-old boy staring down at him with his face covered with grotesque makeup and being forced to kiss the lipstick on his dead mouth. I refused and ran screaming up the aisle of the funeral parlor away from his coffin, his death. The pride and future of our family had been changed into this rouged and lipsticked corpse thing.

It was raining outside.

It was night.

The Japanese people indirectly killed him.

They dropped the bomb on him.

After his love affair with the divorcée in San Francisco, he went up to Sitka, Alaska, to work on the air base.

This is how he died.

He was working on the air base with bandages still wrapped around his head. He had not completely recovered from the effects of the bomb but he wanted to help his country, so he went up there.

One day some lumber was piled on a platform that was being brought up by a crane to the third floor of a building under construction.

He stepped onto the pile of lumber and started going up with it. I guess he had wanted to see somebody or check out something inside the building. When the platform was sixteen feet above the ground, he fell off it and broke his neck.

Thousands of people fall off things sixteen feet

high and walk away from it, shaken up but not hurt. Others break their arms or legs. My uncle Edward broke his neck and was on his way to me standing over his coffin on a rainy night in Tacoma, Washington, being asked to show my love for him by kissing the lipstick on his dead mouth. I refused and ran screaming up the aisle of the funeral parlor.

It was believed that what caused him to fall from the platform was a siege of dizziness related to the effects of the shrapnel entering his skull from the Japanese bomb.

He just got dizzy and fell off and broke his neck.

I once wrote a poem about his death when I was about the same age as my uncle Edward. The poem is called "1942" and goes like this:

> Piano tree, play
> in the dark concert halls
> of my uncle,
> twenty-six years old, dead
> and homeward bound
> on a ship from Sitka,
> his coffin travels
> like the fingers
> of Beethoven
> over a glass
> of wine.
>
> Piano tree, play
> in the dark concert halls
> of my uncle,
> a legend of my childhood, dead,

they send him back
to Tacoma.
At night his coffin
travels like the birds
that fly beneath the sea,
never touching the sky.

Piano tree, play
in the dark concert halls
of my uncle,
take his heart
for a lover
and take his death
for a bed,
and send him homeward bound
on a ship from Sitka
to bury him
where I was born.

Indirectly the Japanese people killed him.
They dropped the bomb on him.
He never really recovered from it.
He has been dead now for thirty-four years.
He was the pride of our family.
He was our future.
Everything that I have just written is a legend of
our family history. Facts and dates may be slightly
off for it was a long time ago, and facts and dates
change. They are altered by the failings of human
memory and embellishment, which is a human trait,
but one thing is totally accurate:
My uncle Edward died in his middle twenties and
he indirectly died as a result of the Japanese people

dropping a bomb on him and nothing in this world, no power or prayer, will ever return him to us.

He is dead.

He is gone forever.

This is a strange way to introduce a book of poetry that expresses my feelings of deep affection for the Japanese people but it has to be done as part of a map that led me to Japan and the writing of this book.

I will continue describing more places on the map that took me to Japan in the late spring of 1976 and these poems.

I hated the Japanese all during the war.

I thought of them as diabolical subhuman creatures that had to be destroyed so that civilization could prevail with liberty and justice for all. In newspaper cartoons they were depicted as buck-toothed monkeys. Propaganda encourages the imagination of children.

I killed thousands of Japanese soldiers playing war. I wrote a short story called "The Ghost Children of Tacoma" that shows my dedication to killing Japanese when I was six, seven, eight, nine and ten years old. I was very good at killing them. They were fun to kill.

During World War II, I personally killed 352,892 enemy soldiers without wounding one. Children need a lot less hospitals in war than grown-ups do. Children pretty much look at it from the alldeath side.

I remember when the war finally ended. I was in a theater watching a Dennis Morgan movie. I think it was a singing foreign legion desert picture but I cannot be certain. Suddenly across the screen came a piece of yellow paper with words typed on it saying that Japan had just surrendered to the United States and World War II was over.

Everybody in the theater started screaming and laughing and were in ecstasy. We rushed out into the streets where car horns were honking. It was a hot summer afternoon. Everything was in Pandemonium. Total strangers were hugging and kissing each other. Every car horn was honking. The streets were flooded with people. All traffic came to a halt. People swarmed kissing each other and laughing like ants over honking cars filled with ecstatic people.

What else could we do?

The long years of war were over.

It was done with. It was ended.

We had defeated and destroyed these subhuman monkeys the Japanese people. Justice and the rights of mankind had triumphed over these creatures that belonged in jungles instead of cities.

I was ten years old.

That's how I felt.

My uncle Edward had been revenged.

His death had been purified by the destruction of Japan.

Hiroshima and Nagasaki were candles burning proudly on the birthday cake of his sacrifice.

Then the years passed.

I grew older.

I was no longer ten.

Suddenly I was fifteen and the war slipped back into memory and my hatred for the Japanese slipped away with it. The emotions began to vaporize.

The Japanese had learned their lesson and being forgiving Christian people we were presenting them with a second chance and they were responding to it splendidly.

We were their father and they were our little children that we had punished severely for being bad but now they were being good and we were forgiving them like good Christians.

After all, they had been subhuman to begin with and now we were teaching them to be human and they were learning very quickly.

The years continued on.

I was seventeen and then eighteen and began to read Japanese haiku poetry from the Seventeenth Century. I read Basho and Issa. I liked the way they used language concentrating emotion, detail and image until they arrived at a form of dew-like steel.

I came to realize that the Japanese people had not been subhuman creatures but had been civilized,

8

feeling and compassionate people centuries before their encounter with us on December 7th.

The war came into focus for me.

I started to understand what had happened.

I began to understand the mechanics which mean that logic and reason fail when war begins and illogic and insanity reign as long as war exists.

I looked at Japanese paintings and scrolls.

I was very impressed.

I liked the way they painted birds because I loved birds and then I was no longer the child of World War II, hating the Japanese, wanting my uncle to be revenged.

I moved to San Francisco and started running around with people who were deeply influenced by and had studied Zen Buddhism. I slowly picked up Buddhism through osmosis by watching the way my friends lived.

I am not a dialectic religious thinker. I have studied very little philosophy.

I watched the way my friends ordered their lives, their houses and handled themselves. I picked up Buddhism like an Indian child learned things before the white man came to America. They learned by watching.

I learned Buddhism by watching.

I learned to love Japanese food and Japanese music. I have seen over five hundred Japanese movies. I learned to read subtitles so fast that I think the actors in the movies are speaking in English.

I had Japanese friends.

I was no longer the hateful boy of my wartime childhood.

My uncle Edward was dead, the pride and future of our family, killed in the prime of life. What were we to do without him?

Over a million young Japanese men, the pride and futures of their families, were also dead, plus hundreds of thousands of innocent women and children who had died in the incendiary raids on Japan and in the atomic bombings of Hiroshima and Nagasaki.

What was Japan to do without them?

I wished that none of it had ever happened.

I read Japanese novels, Tanizaki, etc.

Then I knew that someday I had to go to Japan. That part of my life was ahead of me in Japan. My books had been translated into Japanese and the response was very intelligent. It inspired and gave me the courage to continue on in my own lonely direction of writing like a timber wolf slipping quietly through the woods.

I hate to travel.

Japan is a long ways off.

But I knew that someday I would have to go there. Japan was like a magnet drawing my soul to a place where it had never been before.

One day I got on an airplane and flew across the Pacific Ocean. These poems are what happened after I got off the airplane and stepped foot onto the ground of Japan. The poems are dated and form a kind of diary.

They are different from other poems that I have written. Anyway, I think they are but I am probably the last person in the world to know. The quality of them is uneven but I have printed them all anyway because they are a diary expressing my feelings and emotions in Japan and the quality of life is often uneven.

They are dedicated to my uncle Edward.

They are dedicated to all the Japanese Uncle Edwards whose lives were taken from their bodies between December 7, 1941 and August 14, 1945 when the war ended.

That was thirty-one years ago.

Almost a third of a century has passed.

The war is over.

May the dead rest eternally in peace, waiting for our arrival.

Pine Creek, Montana
August 6, 1976

JUNE 30,th JUNE 30th

Kitty Hawk Kimonos

Watching Japanese television,
two young women in kimonos
are standing beside a biplane.
    That's right:
    an old timey airplane.

A man is interviewing them.
They are having a very animated
and happy conversation.

I wish I knew Japanese because
I will never know why they are
    standing next
    to a biplane,

but they will stand there forever
in my mind, happy pilots
    in their kimonos,
    waiting to take off.

Tokyo
May 13, 1976

15

Crow

This morning I was wondering
when I would see my first bird
   in Japan.
I was betting my mental money
on a sparrow when I heard
   a rooster
   crowing
from a backyard in the Shibuya District
   of Tokyo
and that took care of that.

Tokyo
May 14, 1976

Japanese Children

I just spent the last half-an-hour
watching a Japanese children's program
    on television.
There are millions of us here in Tokyo.
    We know what we like.

Tokyo
May 14, 1976

Cat in Shinjuku

A brown cat lies
in front of a Chinese restaurant
in a very narrow lane
    in Shinjuku.*

The window of the restaurant is
filled with plastic models
of Chinese food that look good
    enough to eat.

The afternoon sun is pleasantly
    warm. The cat
    is enjoying it.

People walk by, very close to the cat
but the cat shows absolutely no fear.
    It does not move.
    I find this unusual.
    The cat is happy
    in front of plastic Chinese
    food with real food
    waiting just inside the door.

Tokyo
The middle of May, 1976

*a large district in Tokyo

The Hillary Express

I just ordered my first meal
    curry and rice
all by myself in a Japanese restaurant.
    What a triumph!
I feel like an infant taking its
    first faltering step.

    Watch out Mount Everest!

Tokyo
May 16, 1976

Kites

A warm Sunday afternoon rainy
4 o'clock back street Ginza
    is closed.

Thousands of napping bars,
their signs are like brightly-colored
    kites.

Wound ball-like narrow streets
and lanes are string.

    quiet
    only a few people
    no wind

Tokyo
May 16, 1976

Japanese Model

Tall, slender
dressed in black
perfect features
Egyptianesque

She is the shadow
of another planet
being photographed
in a totally white room

Her face never changes
her page-boy hair
looks as if it were cut
from black surgical jade

Her lips are so red
they make blood
seem dull, a
useless pastime

Tokyo
May ?, 1976

21

Romance

I just spent fifteen seconds
staring at a Japanese fly:
    my first.

He was standing on a red brick
in the Mitsui Building Plaza,
    enjoying the sun.

He didn't care that I was looking at him.
He was cleaning his face. Perhaps he had
    a date with a beautiful
    lady fly, his bride to be
    or maybe just good friends
    to have lunch a little later
    in Mitsui Plaza
    at noon.

Tokyo
May 17 or 18, 1976

Pachinko Samurai

I feel wonderful, exhilarated, child-like,
    perfect.

I just won two cans of crab meat*
and a locomotive**

What more could anyone ask for on May 18,
    1976 in Tokyo?

I played the game of pachinko
/ vertical pinball /
My blade was sharp.

*real
**toy

Japan

Japan begins and ends
    with Japan.

Nobody else knows the
    story.

. . . Japanese dust
in the Milky Way.

Tokyo
May 18, 1976

Homage to the
Japanese Haiku Poet Issa

Drunk in a Japanese
    bar
    I'm
    OK

Tokyo
May 18, 1976

Dreams Are like the [the]

Dreams are like the [the]
wind. They blow by. The
small ones are breezes,
but they go by, too.

Tokyo
May 20 or 26, 1976

Strawberry Haiku

• • • • •
• • • • • • •
The twelve red berries

Tokyo
May 22, 1976

A Mystery Story or
Dashiell Hammett a la Mode

Every time I leave my hotel room
  here in Tokyo
I do the same four things:
  I make sure I have my passport
  my notebook
  a pen
  and my English–
  Japanese dictionary.

The rest of life is a total mystery.

Tokyo
May 26, 1976

A Short Study in Gone

When dreams wake
    life ends.
Then dreams are gone.
    Life is gone.

Tokyo
May 26, 1976

The 12,000,000

I'm depressed,
haunted by melancholy
that does not have a reflection
    nor cast a shadow.
12,000,000 people live here in Tokyo.
I know I'm not alone.
Others must feel the way
    I do.

Tokyo
May 26, 1976
1 P.M.

Shoes, Bicycle

Listening to the Japanese night,
the window is closed and the curtain pulled,
I think it is raining outside.
It's comforting. I love the rain.
I am in a city that I have never been before:
    Tokyo.
I think it is raining. Then I hear a storm begin.
    I'm slightly drunk:

    people walking by in the street,
    a bicycle.

Tokyo
May 26, 1976

31

A Study in Roads

All the possibilities of life,
all roads led here.

I was never going anyplace else,
    41 years of life:

        Tacoma, Washington
        Great Falls, Montana
        Oaxaca, Mexico
        London, England
        Bee Caves, Texas
        Victoria, British Columbia
        Key West, Florida
        San Francisco, California
        Boulder, Colorado

    all led here:

Having a drink by myself
in a bar in Tokyo before
    lunch,
wishing there was somebody to talk
    to.

Tokyo
May 28, 1976

Floating Chandeliers

Sand is crystal
like the soul.
The wind blows
it away.

Tokyo
May 28, 1976

33

Japanese Women

If there are any unattractive
    Japanese women
they must drown them at birth.

Tokyo
May 28, 1976

Taxi Drivers Look Different from Their Photographs

There is no difference
between Tokyo and New York.
These men do not look
like their photographs.
These are different men.
I'm not being fooled in the
least. Complete strangers drive
    these cabs.

Tokyo
May 28, 1976

35

Sunglasses Worn at Night in Japan

A Japanese woman
    age: 28

lives seeing darkness
    from eyes

that should see light
    at night.

Tokyo
May 30, 1976

Japanese Pop Music Concert

Don't *ever ever* forget
    the flowers
that were rejected, made
    fools of.

A very shy girl gives the
budding boy pop star a bouquet
    of beautiful
    flowers

between songs. What courage
it took for her to walk up to
the stage and hand him the
    flowers.

He puts them garbage-like down
on the floor. They lie there.
She returns to her seat and watches
    her flowers lying there.
Then she can't take it any longer.

    She flees.
    She is gone
    but the music
    plays on.

    I promise.
    You promise, too

Tokyo
May 31, 1976

37

Future

Ah, June 1, 1976
   12:01 A.M.

All those who live
after we are dead

We knew this moment
   we were here

Tokyo
June 1, 1976
12:01 A.M.

Talking

I am the only American in this bar.
Everybody else is Japanese.
  (reasonable / Tokyo)

I speak English.
They speak Japanese.
  (of course)

They try to speak English. It's hard.
I can't speak any Japanese. I can't help.
We talk for a while, trying.

Then they switch totally to Japanese
    for ten minutes.
They laugh. They are serious.
They pause between words.

I am alone again. I've been there before
in Japan, America, everywhere when you
don't understand what somebody is
    talking about.

Tokyo
June 1, 1976

Chainsaw

A beautiful Japanese woman
   / age 42

the energy that separates
   spring from summer

      (depending on June)
      20 or 21
      —so they say—

Her voice singing sounds
just like an angelic chainsaw
   cutting through
   honey.

Tokyo
June 1, 1976

Day for Night

The cab takes me home
through the Tokyo dawn.
I have been awake all night.
I will be asleep before the sun
    rises.
I will sleep all day.
The cab is a pillow,
the streets are blankets,
the dawn is my bed.
The cab rests my head.
I'm on my way to dreams.

Tokyo
June 1, 1976

41

Cobalt Necessity

It's just one of those things.
When you need cobalt
    nothing else will
        suffice.

Tokyo
June 2, 1976

Real Estate

I have emotions
that are like newspapers that
    read themselves.

I go for days at a time
trapped in the want ads.

I feel as if I am an ad
for the sale of a haunted house:

    18 rooms
    $37,000
    I'm yours
    ghosts and all.

Tokyo
June 2, 1976

43

The Alps

One word

waiting . . .

leads to an
avalanche
of other words

if you are

waiting . . .

for a woman

Tokyo
June 2, 1976

Japan Minus Frogs

For Guy de la Valdene

Looking casually
through my English–Japanese dictionary
I can't find the word frog.
   It's not there.
Does that mean that Japan has no frogs?

Tokyo
June 4, 1976

On the Elevator Going Down

A Caucasian gets on at
    the 17th floor.
He is old, fat and expensively
    dressed.

I say hello / I'm friendly.
    He says, "Hi."

Then he looks very carefully at
    my clothes.

I'm not expensively dressed.
I think his left shoe costs more
than everything I am wearing.

He doesn't want to talk to me
    any more.

I think that he is not totally aware
that we are really going down
and there are no clothes after you have
been dead for a few thousand years.

He thinks as we silently travel
down and get off at the bottom
    floor
that we are going separate
    ways.

Tokyo
June 4, 1976

A Young Japanese Woman Playing a Grand Piano in an Expensive and Very Fancy Cocktail Lounge

Everything shines like black jade:

> The piano (invented
> Her long hair (severe
> Her obvious disinterest (in the music
>> she is playing.

Her mind, distant from her fingers,
is a million miles away shining

> like black
> jade

Tokyo
June 4, 1976

A Small Boat on the Voyage of Archaeology

A warm thunder and lightning storm
tonight in Tokyo with lots of rain and umbrellas
    around 10 P.M.
This is a small detail right now
but it could be very important
a million years from now when archaeologists
sift through our ruins, trying to figure us
    out.

Tokyo
June 5, 1976

American Bar in Tokyo

I'm here in a bar filled with
young conservative snobbish
    American men,
drinking and trying to pick up
    Japanese women
who want to sleep with the likes
    of these men.
It is very hard to find any poetry
    here
as this poem bears witness.

Tokyo
June 5, 1976

Ego Orgy on a Rainy Night in Tokyo
with Nobody to Make Love to

The night is now
half-gone; youth
goes; I am

in bed alone

      —Sappho

My books have been translated
    into
Norwegian, French, Danish, Romanian,
Spanish, Japanese, Dutch, Swedish,
Italian, German, Finnish, Hebrew
    and published in England

      but

I will sleep alone tonight in Tokyo
    raining.

          Tokyo
          June 5, 1976

Worms

The distances of loneliness
make the fourth dimension
seem like three hungry crows
looking at a worm in a famine.

Tokyo
June 6, 1976

Things to Do on a Boring Tokyo Night in a Hotel

1. Have dinner by yourself.
    That's always a lot of fun.

2. Wander aimlessly around the hotel.
    This is a huge hotel, so there's lots of space
    to wander aimlessly around.

3. Go up and down the elevator for no reason
        at all.
    The people going up are going to their rooms.
        I'm not.
    Those going down are going out.
        I'm not.

4. I seriously think about the house phone
    and calling my room 3003 and letting it ring
    for a very long time. Then wondering where
    I'm at and when I will return. Should I leave
    a message at the desk saying that when I return
        I should call myself?

Tokyo
June 6, 1976

Travelling toward Osaka
on the Freeway from Tokyo

I look out the car window
at 100 kilometers an hour
        (62 miles)
and see a man peddling
a bicycle very carefully
down a narrow path between
        rice paddies.
He's gone in a few seconds.
I have only his memory now.
He has been changed into
a 100 kilometer-an-hour
memory ink rubbing.

Hamamatsu
June 7, 1976

After the Performance of the
Black Tent Theater Group on the Shores
of the Nagara River

The actresses without their make-up,
their costumes, their roles
are returned to being mortals.
I watch them eat quietly in a small inn.
They have no illusions, almost plain
    like saints,
    perfect in their
    re-entry.

Gifu
June 7, 1976

Fragment #1

Speaking is speaking
when you *(The next word is unintelligible,*
written on a drunken scrap of paper.)

speak any more.

Tokyo
Perhaps a day in early
June

Lazarus on the Bullet Train

For Tagawa Tadasu

*The Bullet Train is the famous Japanese express
train that travels 120 miles an hour. Lazarus is an
old stand-by.*

You listened to the ranting and raving drunken
American writer on the Bullet Train from Nagoya
as I blamed you for everything that ever went
wrong in this world, including the grotesque
event that occurred that night in Gifu while
　　　you slept.

Of course, you had done nothing but be my good
friend. At one point I told you to consider me
dead, that I was dead for you from that moment on.
I took your hand and touched my hand with it.
I told you that my flesh was now cold to you:
　　　dead.

You silently nodded your head, eyes filled
with sadness. I even forbid you to ever read
one of my books again because I knew how much
you loved them and again you nodded your head
and you didn't say anything. The sadness in your
　　　eyes did all the speaking.

56

The Bullet Train continued travelling at 120
miles an hour back to Tokyo as I ranted and raved
    at you.

You didn't say a word.
Your sadness filled the Bullet Train
with two hundred extra passengers.
They were all reading newspapers
that had no words printed on them,
only the dried tears of the dead.

By the time the train reached Tokyo Station,
my anger had turned slowly and was headed in all
directions toward a deserved oblivion.
I took your hand and touched my hand again.
"I'm alive for you," I said. "The warmth has
    returned to my flesh."

You nodded silently again,
never having said a word.
The two hundred extra passengers
remained on the train,
though it was the end of the line.
They will stay there forever riding
back and forth until they are dust.
We stepped out into the early Tokyo morning
    friends again.

Oh, thank you, Tagawa Tadasu,
O beautiful human being for sharing

and understanding my death
and return from the dead
on the Bullet Train between Nagoya
    and Tokyo the morning of June 8, 1976.

Later in the evening I called you
on the telephone. Your first
words were: "Are you fine?"
    "Yes, I am fine."

Tokyo
June 9, 1976

Visiting a Friend at the Hospital

I just visited Kazuko at the hospital.
She seemed tired. She was operated on
  six days ago.
She ate her dinner slowly, painfully.
It was sad to watch her eat. She was
very tired. I wish that I could have
eaten in her place and she to receive
  the nutriment.

Tokyo
June 9, 1976

Eternal Lag

Before flying to Japan
I was worried about jet lag.

"My" airplane would leave
San Francisco at 1 P.M.
    Wednesday
and 10 hours and 45 minutes later
would land in Tokyo at 4 P.M.
    the next day:
    Thursday.

I was worried about that,
forgetting that because I suffer
from severe insomnia I have
    eternal jet lag.

Tokyo
June 9, 1976

The American in Tokyo with a Broken Clock

For Shiina Takako

People stare at me—
There are millions of them.
Why is this strange American
walking the streets of early night
    carrying a broken clock
        in his hands?
Is he for real or is he just an illusion?
How the clock got broken is not important.
    Clocks break.
    Everything breaks.
People stare at me and the broken clock
    that I carry like a dream

    in my hands.

Tokyo
June 10, 1976

The American Fool

A few weeks ago a middle-aged taxi driver
started talking to me in English. His English
    was very good.
I asked him if he had ever been to America.
Wordlessly, poignantly he made a motion
with his hand that was not driving the streets
    of Tokyo
at his face that suddenly looked very sad.
The gesture meant that he was a poor man
and would never be able to afford to go to America.
We didn't talk much after that.

                Tokyo
            June 11, 1976

The American Carrying a Broken Clock in Tokyo Again

For Shiina Takako

It is amazing how many people
you meet when you are carrying
a broken clock around in Tokyo.

Today I was carrying the broken clock
around again, trying to get an exact
    replacement for it.
    The clock was far beyond repair.

All sorts of people were interested
in the clock. Total strangers came up to me
and inquired about the clock in Japanese
    of course
and I nodded my head: Yes, I have a broken clock.

I took it to a restaurant and people gathered
around. I recommend carrying a broken clock
with you at all times if you want to meet new
friends. I think it would work anyplace in the
    world.

    If you want to go to Iceland
    and meet the people, take
    a broken clock with you.
    They will gather around like flies.

Tokyo
June 11, 1976

The Nagara, the Yellowstone

Fish rise in the early summer evenings
on the Nagara River at Gifu. I am back in Tokyo.
I will never fish the Nagara. The fish
will rise there forever but the Yellowstone River
south of Livingston, Montana, that is another
     story.

Tokyo
June 11, 1976

Writing Poetry in Public Places, Cafes, Bars, Etc.

Alone in a place full of strangers
I sing as if I'm in the center
    of a heavenly choir

    —my tongue a cloud of honey—

Sometimes I think I'm weird.

Tokyo
June 11, 1976

Cashier

The young Japanese woman cashier,
 who doesn't like me
 I don't know why
 I've done nothing to her except exist,
uses a calculator to add up the checks
at a speed that approaches light—

clickclickclickclickclickclickclickclick
 she adds up her dislike
  for me.

        Tokyo
        June 11, 1976

Tokyo / June 11, 1976

I have the five poems
that I wrote earlier today
    in a notebook
in the same pocket that
I carry my passport. They
are the same thing.

Meiji Comedians

For Shiina Takako

Meiji Shrine is Japan's most famous shrine.
Emperor Meiji and his consort Empress Shôken are
enshrined there. The grounds occupy 175 acres of
gardens, museums and stadiums.

Meiji Shrine was closed.
We snuck in the hour before dawn.
We were drunk like comedians
climbing over stone walls and falling down.
We were funny to watch.
Fortunately, the police did not discover us
    and take us away.
It was beautiful there and we staggered
around in the trees and bushes until light started.
We were very funny and then
we were lying sprawled in a small meadow
of gentle green grass that was sweet
    to the touch of our bodies.
I put my hand on her breast and started kissing
her. She kissed me back and that's all the love
we made. We didn't go any further, but it was
perfect in the early light of Meiji Shrine

with the Emperor Meiji
and his consort Empress Shôken
somewhere near us.

Tokyo
June 12, 1976

Meiji Shoes Size 12

For Shiina Takako

I woke up in the middle of the afternoon, alone,
our love-making did not lead to going to bed
together and that was OK, I guess.

Beside the bed were my shoes covered with Meiji
mud. I looked at them and felt very good.
It's funny what the sight of dried mud can do
    to your mind.

Tokyo
June 12, 1976

Starting

Starting just a single world

*start (start) v.i. 1, begin or enter
upon an action, etc; set out.*

to end with.

*Tokyo
June 12, 1976*

Passing to Where?

Sometimes I take out my passport,
look at the photograph of myself
    (not very good, etc.)

    just to see if I exist

Tokyo
June 12, 1976

Tokyo / June 13, 1976

I have sixteen more days left in Japan.
I leave on the 29th back across the Pacific.
Five days after that I will be in Montana,
sitting in the stands of the Park County
    Fairgrounds,

watching the Livingston Roundup
    on the Fourth of July,
    cheering the cowboys on,

    Japan gone.

The Airplane

                        One
of the bad things about staying at a hotel
is the thin walls. They are a problem
that does not go away. I was trying to get
some sleep this afternoon but the people
in the next room took that opportunity to
        fuck their brains out.
Their bed sounded like an old airplane
        warming up to take off.
I lay there a few feet away, trying to get
some sleep while their bed taxied down the
        runway.

                              Tokyo
                              June 14, 1976

Orson Welles

Orson Welles does whisky commercials on Japanese television. It's strange to see him here on television in Tokyo, recommending that the Japanese people buy G & G Nikka whisky.

I always watch him with total fascination. Last night I dreamt that I directed one of the commercials. There were six black horses in the commercial.

The horses were arranged in such a position that upon seeing them and Orson Welles together, people would rush out of their homes and buy G & G Nikka whisky.

It was not an easy commercial to film. It had to be perfect. It took many takes. Mr. Welles was very patient with an understanding sense of humor.

"Please, Mr. Welles," I would say. "Stand a little closer to the horses."

He would smile and move a little closer to the horses.

"How's this?"

"Just fine, Mr. Welles, perfect."

Tokyo
June 14, 1976

The Red Chair

I saw a decadent gothic Japanese movie
this evening. It went so far beyond any
decadence that I have ever seen before
that I was transformed into a child learning
                    for the first time
        that shadows are not always friendly,
        that houses are haunted,
        that people sometimes have thoughts
        made out of snake skin that crawl
        toward the innocence of sleeping babies.

The movie took place in Tokyo
just before the earthquake on September 1, 1923.
In a gothic Japanese house a man was hiding
inside a large stuffed red chair while a beautiful
woman wearing exotic costumes made love
to other men sitting in the chair.
The men did not know that somebody was hiding
        inside the chair,
feeling, voyeuring every detail of their passion.
It took a long time in the movie
before I realized that there was a man inside the
        chair.

The film went on and on into decadence
after decadence like a rainbow of perversion.
I can't describe them all.
You would have trouble believing them.

The red chair was only a beginning.

I sat there transfixed
with a hundred Japanese men.
It was as if we were the orgasm
of spiders fucking in dried human
    blood.

Tokyo
June 15, 1976

The Silence of Language

                                    I'm
sitting here awkwardly alone in a bar
with a very intelligent Japanese movie director
who can't speak English and I no Japanese.

We know each other but there is nobody here
to translate for us. We've talked before.
Now we pretend to be interested in other things.

He is listening to some music on the phonograph
with his eyes closed. I am writing this down.
It's time to go home. He leaves first.

Tokyo
June 15, 1976

It's Time to Wake Up

I set the alarm for 9 A.M.
but it wasn't necessary.
The earthquake at 7:30 woke
    me up.

From the middle of a dream
I was suddenly lying there
feeling the hotel shake,
wondering if room 3003
would soon be a Shinjuku
    intersection
      30 floors below.

It sure beats the hell
out of an alarm clock.

Tokyo
June 16, 1976

Fragment #2 / Having

I found the word *having* written sideways,
    all by itself
on a piece of notebook paper.
I have no idea why I wrote it
or what its ultimate destination was,
but I wrote the word *having* very carefully

    and then stopped

    writing.

Tokyo
June perhaps, 1976

Looking at My Bed / 3 A.M.

Sleep without sleep,
then to sleep again
    without
    sleeping.

Tokyo
June 17, 1976

Taxi Driver

I like this taxi driver,
racing through the dark streets
    of Tokyo
as if life had no meaning.
I feel the same way.

Tokyo
June 17, 1976
10 P.M.

Taking No Chances

I am a part of it. No,
I am the total but there
is also a possibility
that I am only a fraction
    of it.

I am that which begins
but has no beginning.
I am also full of shit
right up to my ears.

Tokyo
June 17, 1976

Tokyo / June 24, 1976

As these poems progress
can you guess June 24, 1976?

I was born January 30, 1935
in Tacoma, Washington.

What will happen next?
If only I could see June 24,
    1976.

Tokyo
June 18, 1976

What Makes Reality Real

Waiting for her . . .
Nothing to do but write a poem.
She is now 5 minutes late.

I have a feeling that she will be at least
    15 minutes late.
It is now 6 minutes after 9 P.M.
    in Tokyo.

    —NOW exactly NOW—
    the doorbell rang.

She is at the door:
6 minutes after 9 P.M.
    in Tokyo

nothing has changed
except that she is here.

Tokyo
June 19, 1976

Unrequited Love

Stop in /
write a morose poem /
leave / if only
life were that easy

Tokyo
June 19, 1976

The Past Cannot Be Returned

The umbilical cord
cannot be refastened
and life flow through it
    again.

Our tears never totally
    dry.

Our first kiss is now a ghost,
haunting our mouths as they
    fade toward
    oblivion.

Tokyo
June 19, 1976
with a few words
added in Montana
July 12, 1976

Fragment #3

speaking is speaking

We repeat
what we speak
and then we are
speaking again and that
speaking is speaking.

Tokyo
June sometime, 1976

Two Women

/ 1

Travelling along
a freeway in Tokyo
I saw a woman's face
reflected back to us
from a small circular mirror
on the passenger side
of the car in front of us.
The car had a regular
rearview mirror in the center
of the front window.

I wondered what the
circular mirror was doing
on the passenger side of the car.
Her face was in it. She was directly
in front of us. She had a beautiful
face, floating in an
unreal mirror on a Tokyo
    freeway.

Her face stayed there for a while
and then floated off
forever in the changing traffic.

She moves like a ghost.
She is not alive any more.
She must be in her late sixties.
She is short and squat
like a Japanese stereotype.

She takes care of the lobby
of the hotel. She empties
the ashtrays. She dusts
and mops things. She moves
like a ghost. She has no human
    expression.

A few days ago I was standing
beside three Japanese businessmen
peeing in the lavatory.
We each had our own urinal.
She walked in like a ghost and started
mopping the toilet floor around us.
She was totally unaware of us,
standing there urinating.
She was truly a ghost
and we were suddenly ghost pee-ers
    as she mopped on
        by.

Tokyo
June 21, 1976

Fragment #4

in a garden of
    500 mossy, lichen
    green Buddhas

a sunny day

    these Buddhas
    know the answer
    to all five
    hundred other Buddhas

                    Never finished
                    outside of Tokyo
                    June 23, 1976
                    except for the word
                    other added at
                    Pine Creek, Montana,
                    on July 23, 1976

91

Illicit Love

We did not play the game.
We played the rules perfectly,
no violations, no penalties.

> The game is over
> or is it just
> beginning?

Tokyo
June 28, 1976

Age: 41

Playing games
playing games, I
guess I never
really stopped
being a child
playing games
playing games

Tokyo
June 28, 1976

93

Two Versions of the Same Poem

Love / 1

The water
in the river
flows over
and under
itself.

It knows
what to do,
flowing on.

Love / 2

The water
in the river
flows over
and under
itself.

It knows
what to do,
flowing on.

The bed never
touches bottom.

Tokyo
June 28, 1976

Stone (real

I guess I moved to Texas:
Bee Caves on the map.
The map means nothing
to you sitting here watching
    me.

                Tokyo
                June 29, 1976
                Very drunk
                with Shiina
                Takako watching
                me

Land of the Rising Sun

sayonara

Flying from Japanese night,
we left Haneda Airport in Tokyo
four hours ago at 9:30 P.M.
    June 30th
and now we are flying into the sunrise
over the Pacific that is on its way
    to Japan
where darkness lies upon the land
and the sun is hours away.
I greet the sunrise of July 1st
for my Japanese friends,
wishing them a pleasant day.
The sun is on its
    way.

> *June 30th again*
> *above the Pacific*
> *across the international date line*
> *heading home to America*
> *with part of my heart*
> *in Japan*

97

RICHARD BRAUTIGAN is forty-three years old and has written eighteen books. He is an internationally-known author whose work has been translated into fifteen languages, including eight books that have been translated into Japanese.